REGGIE & ROCKY
The Ring-tailed Raccoons

AUTHOR: MARY FLYNN
ILLUSTRATED BY DONNA CRAFT

Published by Barlemarry Press, Apopka, FL, 2018

Cover art and illustrations by Donna Craft » dcraftmountdora@gmail.com
Cover design, backgrounds & layout by Michael Butler » www.TorqueCreativeLLC.com

Dedicated to Joanie Hoffman, who introduced me to her noisy little visitors.

the ring-tailed raccoons,

Came out of the woods

by the fullest of moons,

That hearing the two of them enter was hard.

Now Reggie and Rocky
                     were hungry, no doubt;

That's why I decided to put some food out,

But what do you feed
                    to a ring-tailed raccoon?

I figured on dog food,
                    but then changed my tune.

For Reggie and Rocky were raccoons not dogs.

Not kittens or squirrels or sparrows or hogs.

So they wouldn't eat carrots or acorns or nuts,

No pine cones, no berries,
        no ifs, ands or buts.

Now I said to myself this is going too far;

Just who do these two raccoons
                    think that they are.

They'll eat what I eat – the very same stuff;

They'll eat it or starve – enough is enough!

So, I put out some broccoli,

beans and spaghetti,

Leftover meatloaf and apple brown betty,

Tacos and marmalade, oatmeal and chili;

The two of them gobbled it up, willy-nilly.

they came the next night,

And I put out some dinner rolls,
whole wheat not white;

Sesame chicken and raspberry tarts.

They snortled it down
                with a raccoon-like snortle,

And relished it so
                that I couldn't help chortle,

For Reggie and Rocky
                    were quite clearly hooked

On all of the food I so skillfully cooked.

Now Reggie and Rocky
                        are great friends of mine;

They come back each evening
                        at midnight to dine.

They eat all my food, no ifs, ands or buts;

Now I'm the one eating the acorns and nuts!

THE END

MARY FLYNN

Mary Flynn is an award-winning author of poetry and fiction, as well as a former international conference speaker for Disney. Her stories are an eclectic and imaginative mix of humor, pathos and irony that explore the human experience, often with a surprising twist.

Mary started her writing career as a full-time staff writer for Hallmark Cards in Kansas City and later became a writer and editor for the leading publisher of stories and comprehension tests used throughout the U.S. public school system.

Her observational humor has appeared in the Sunday *New York Times*, *Newsday* and other dailies and magazines. *Reggie & Rocky, The Ring-tailed Raccoons* and *Reggie & Rocky, The Naughty Raccoons* are the first two books in her playfully rhymed raccoon series. *Mrs. Peppel's Pillows*, a novella for middle-grade readers, was a finalist in the Royal Palm Literary Awards.

She recently released her poetry collection along with a book on Disney leadership, *Disney's "Secret Sauce": The Little-known Factor Behind The Business World's Most Legendary Leadership*. Her Gold Medal debut novel, *Margaret Ferry*, is rated five-stars on Amazon.

Mary was a *Writer's Digest* poetry winner. She was also honored as a Royal Palm Literary Awards winner for her short story, "Jeremiah's Orchard," which appeared in *The Saturday Evening Post's Anthology of Great American Fiction*. Mary enjoys entertaining audiences with her unique program, "Confessions of a Hallmark Greeting Card Writer," and loves speaking to book clubs.

Read more at **maryflynnwrites.com**. and **maryflynnwrites.growingbolder.com**.

Contact Mary at **mflynn7@cfl.rr.com**

DONNA CRAFT

An amazing artist whose quirky and imaginative illustrations have delighted a generation of readers of children's books, as well as collectors of bright and visually compelling art.

A master of whimsy, color and design, Donna swiftly and flawlessly interprets the story with her signature style. Her dynamic illustrations enrich every story and captivate readers, young and old alike.

Contact Donna at **dcraftmountdora@gmail.com**

ABOUT RACCOONS

Most people know raccoons as cute little animals who come at night to tear open trash bags and knock over garbage cans looking for food. Raccoons will eat almost anything, but they especially like fruits, plants, frogs and rodents, such as mice and rats. They also snatch bird eggs from their nests.

It often surprises people to find out that raccoons are also very good at hunting in water. They are quick enough to catch crayfish and other little water creatures.

Raccoons live throughout the United States, as well as Canada, Mexico and some parts of Europe. They are easy to spot because of the black markings around their eyes that make them look like they are wearing a mask. Many raccoons also have rings around their tails.

Raccoons have five toes on their front paws, making it easy to handle their food. They can even use their toes to turn doorknobs and open door latches.

Raccoons weigh about as much as some dogs, roughly between fourteen and twenty-five pounds. The male raccoon is called a boar, the female is called a sow, and a young raccoon is called a kit. Raccoons can live as long as twenty years.

Raccoons often live in a tree hole or a hollowed out log. They can even live in the attic of a house, which can be dangerous for people because raccoons do not make good pets. They can use their front paws as weapons and they often carry diseases harmful to humans.

Raccoons are beautiful creatures and can be fun to watch from a safe distance.

Don't miss out on the fun!
Get both Reggie & Rocky books.

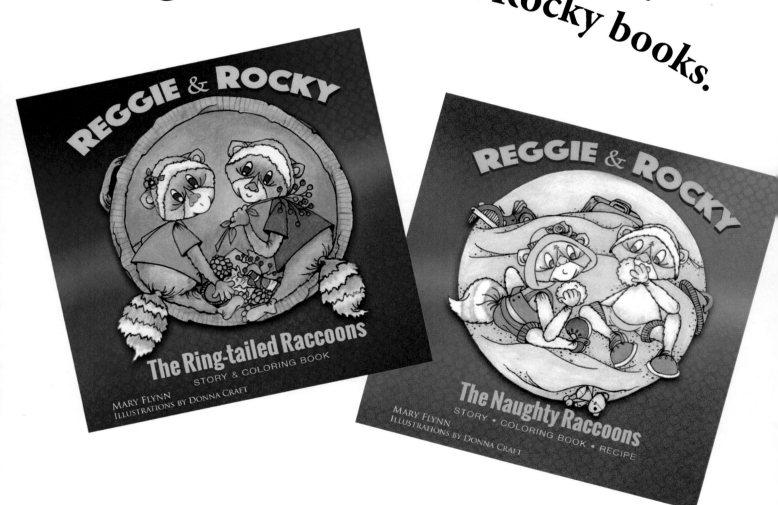

Made in the USA
Middletown, DE
24 February 2024

50147371R00029